Sheep	Duck	Horse
🏴 BAA BAA	🏴 QUACK QUACK	🏴 NEIGH NEIGH
BEE BEE	CWAC CWAC	
BA BA	WAC WAC	
МПЕЕЕ МПЕЕЕ (BEEE BEEE)	KOYAK KOYAK (KUAK KUA...	
BEEH BEEH	QUA QUA	
BE BE	QUAC QUAC	
BEH BEH	COIN COIN	HIIII
BEEE	CUA CUA	IIIII
BEE BEE	QUAC QUAC	IIII
BAAY BAAY	QUEN QUEN	YAHOU
BEEE	MAC MAC	EE-HAHA
MAY MAY	BRA BRA BRA	HO HO HO
BUYUY BUYUY	KVAKK KVAKK	VRINSK VRINSK
MEH MEH	RAP RAP	VRINSK VRINSK
BE BE	KVACK KVACK	GNEGG GNEGG
MA	KWAK KWAK	HEHEHEHE
BLE BLE	KWAHK KWAHK	RINNEK RINNEK
MAYH MAYH	QUAK QUAK	IHAHAHAAA
BĒĒ (BEH)	PĒK PĒK (PEHK PEHK)	IJĀ (IYA)
BEE BEE	KWA KWA	EHA HA
BE BE	KWAK KWAK	HI HI
BAA	GA GA	EEHAHA
BEH BEH	GA GA	EHAHA
БЕЕЕ (BEEE)	КВА КВА (KWA KWA)	ЊИИИИИ (NYEEEE)
БЕЕ БЕЕ (BA BA)	ПА ПА (KFA KFA)	ИИИ ИИИИ (EEE EEEEEE)
Б-Е-Е-Е (B-EH-EH-EH-EH)	КРЯ КРЯ (KRA KRA)	И ГО ГО (EE-JO-JO)
БЕ-Е (BEH-EH)	КРЯ КРЯ (KRA KRA)	IГО ГО (EEJO-JO)
БЯ БЯ (BYA BYA)	ВЯРК ВЯРК (WYARK WYARK)	ЦЯ Я (TSYA-A)
MEHH MEHH	PREHKS PREHKS	EEHA-HAA
MEHH MEHH	KFAAK KFAAK	EEHAHAA
BEEE	HAWP HAWP	NUEEHAHA
BEH	GA GA	EHAHA
מֶה מֶה (MEEE MEEE)	נֶע נֶע (GA GA)	אִי-הִי-הִי (E-HEE-HEE)
ثغاء (THUGHAA)	زبط (ZABAT)	صهيل (SAHEEL)
بَع بَع (BAY BAY)	قاد قاد (GHAD GHAD)	ای ها ها (I-HA-HA)
भ्याँ भ्याँ (BAA BAA)		हिनहिन (HEENHEEN)
咩 咩 (MIE MIE)		嘶 嘶 (TZEE TZEE)
メ— (MEH)		ヒヒーン (HEHEE-N)
–		힝힝 (HEE HEE)
EMBEK		RINGKIKAN
BAA BAA	KUACK KUACK	NAIGH NAIGH

Bee	Cow	Pig
BUZZ BUZZ	MOO	OINK OINK
SUO SUO	MW	RHOCH RHOCH
BIS BIS	MOO MOO	AHNC AHNC
ΜΠZZZ ΜΠZZZ (BSSS BSSS)	ΜΟΥΟΥ (MOU)	OINK OINK
ZZZ	MUUH MUUH	GRUNF GRUNF
BSSS BSSS	MU MU	GRUGN GRUGN
BZZZ	MEUH	GROIN GROIN
BZZZ	MUUU	OINC OINC
ZZZ	MUU	NYEE NYEE
BZZ BZZ	MUUU	OINK OINK
BZZZ	MUU MUU	GUIȚ GUIȚ (GUIT GUIT)
BEEUM BEUM	BOO BOO	GRONK GRONK
SUM SUM	MEU MEU	NAWFF NAWFF
SUM SUM	MUH MUH	AWF AWF
SURR SURR	MU	NAWF NAWF
ZOEM ZOEM	BOW	KNOR KNOR
ZOOM ZOOM	MOOO	OINK OINK
SUM SUM SUM	MOOH MOOH	OINK OINK
ZUMM ZUMM	MŪ (MOO)	RUK RUK
BZZZ	MUU	KRUM KRUM
BZZZ	BOOO	KRR KRR
BZZZ	MUU	–
ZU ZU	MU MU	ROK ROK
ЗЗЗЗЗЗЗЗ (SSSSSSSS)	МУУУ (MUUU)	СКВИ СКВИ (SKWI SKWI)
БЪЗЗЗ (BSSS)	МУУ МУУ (MOO MOO)	ГРУХ ГРУХ (GROOH GROOH)
БЗЗЗ (BSSS)	МУУ (MOO-OO)	ХРЮ ХРЮ (HRYOO HRYOO)
БЗЗЗ (BSSS)	МУУ (MOO-OO)	ХРЮ (HRYOO)
БЪЗ БЪЗ (BS BS)	ПА АР (PAH-AH)	РОХ РОХ (ROH ROH)
ZUM ZUM	AMOOOO	RUIK RUIK
SURRRR	AMOO	RUH RUH
ZUM ZUM	BOOO	RUF RUF
ZUM ZUM	MU	–
בְּזְזז (BSSS)	מוּוו (MOOO)	אוֹינְק אוֹינְק (OINK OINK)
طنين (TANEEN)	خوار (KUVAAR)	خفخفة (KHAFAKHAFA)
ویز (WEES)	هوم (HOOM)	خر خر (KHOR KHOR)
भी भी (SI SI)	मु (MIOW MIOW)	गुर गुर (GUR GUR)
嗡 嗡 (VENG VENG)	哞 (MOU)	呼 噜 (HOO-YOO)
ブゥーン (BOON)	モォー (MOO)	ブーブー (BOO BOO)
ผึ้ง (FEE)	มอ มอ (MO MO)	อู๊ด อู๊ด (UD UD)
DENGUNG	LENGOO	DENGOOS
BEUZZZ BEUZZZ	MOOO	TWEE TWEE

Everyone knows that people from different countries, regions, or even different towns sometimes speak different languages, but did you ever wonder about animals? Well, they are just the same! Take a look at the three sheep above. Do you think they understand each other? I doubt it. Without learning foreign animal languages, they'll never be able to talk to each other and exchange important sheep thoughts with other sheep from around the world. You can use this book to teach your animals how to speak in different languages.

Check out the pronunciation guides at the front and the back of this book to see how to talk to 14 different animals in 41 different languages. That's 574 animal words! The guide is written phonetically so you'll know just how to say each one!

Special thanks to all my friends,
who voluntarily helped me to create this book.
—Lila Prap

Animals Speak

Lila Prap

NORTH-SOUTH BOOKS / NEW YORK / LONDON

Portuguese   IÒ

Catalan   IHÀ

Farsi   ای یا

The sheep bleats:

BAA

The duck quacks:
QUACK

	Hungarian	HÁP
	Czech	KVÁK
	Bulgarian	ПА

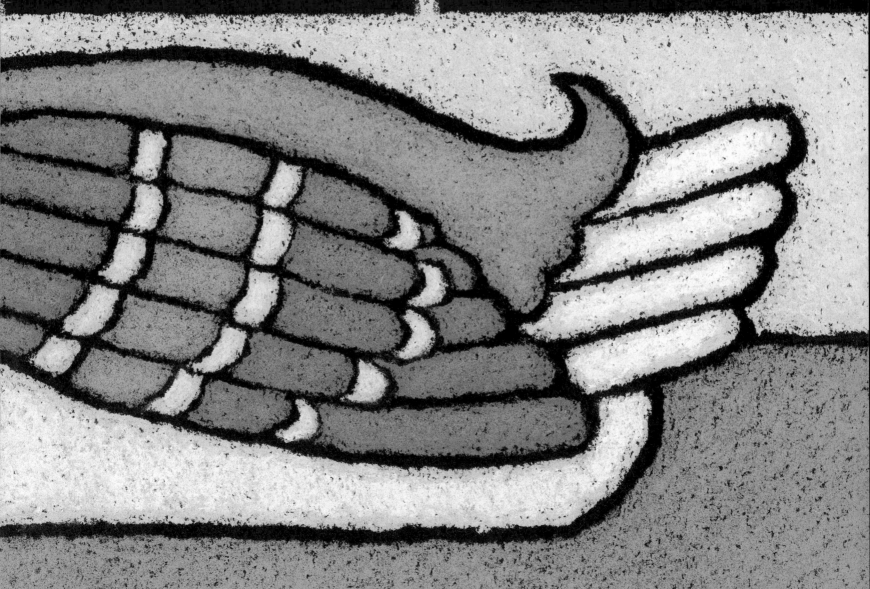

The horse neighs:

NEIGH

In Welsh I say:

NEI

	Portuguese	**YAHOU**
	Arabic	صهيل
	Danish	**VRINSK**

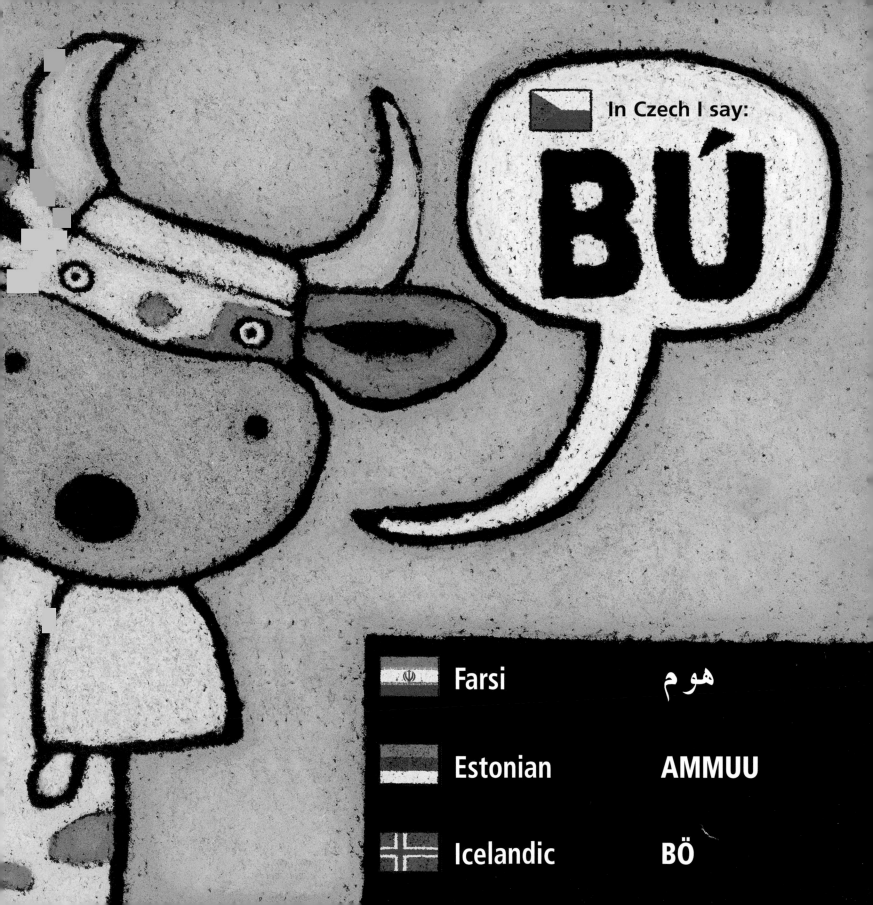

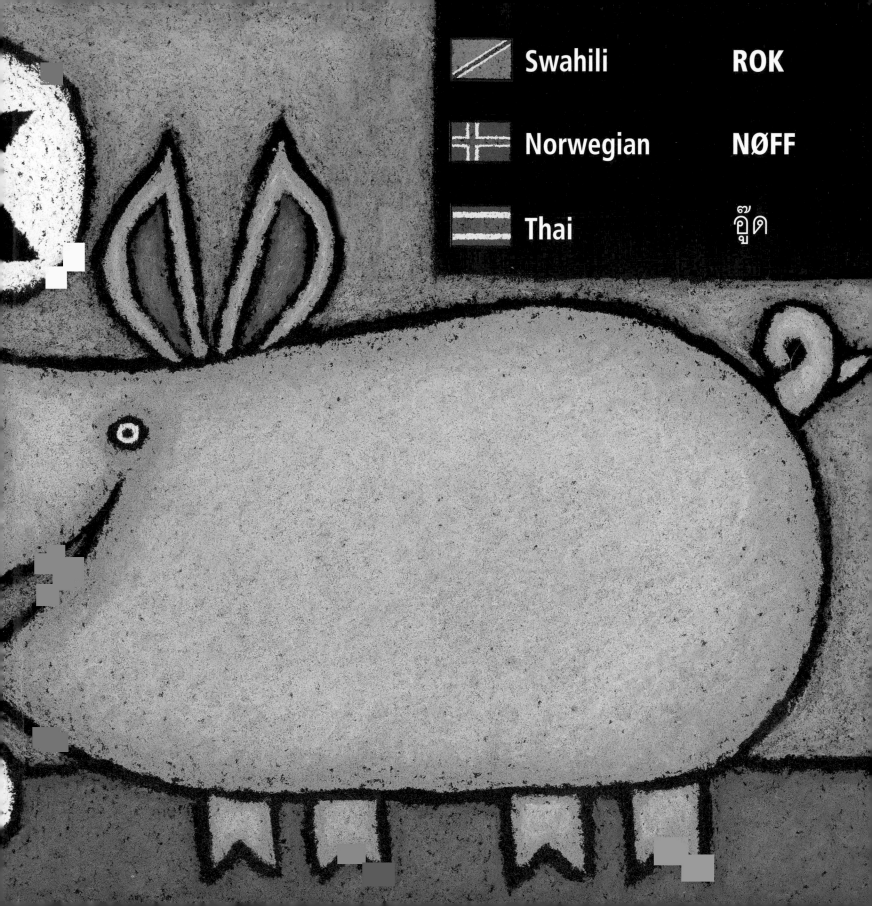

Swahili **ROK**

Norwegian **NØFF**

Thai อู๊ด

In Irish I say:

ÍDHEABH

	Latvian	**NAU**
	Hebrew	מְיָאוּ
	Ukrainian	МЯУ

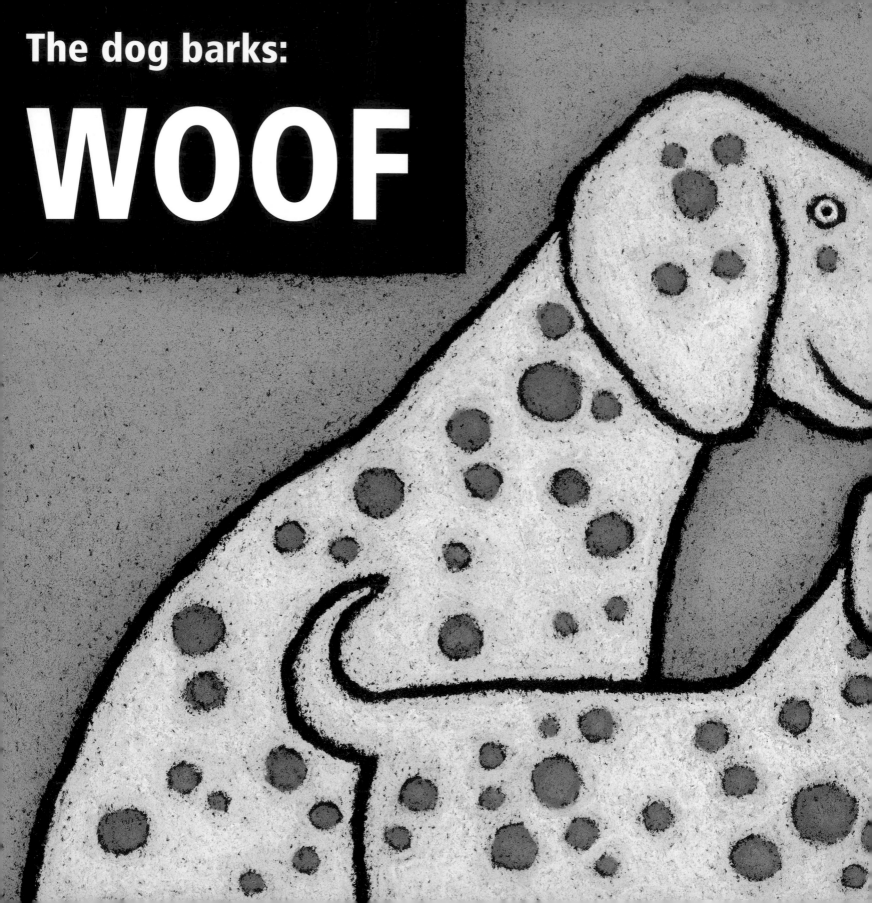

The dog barks:

WOOF

Romanian **CIRIP**

Italian **CIP**

Mokshan **ЦИЙ**

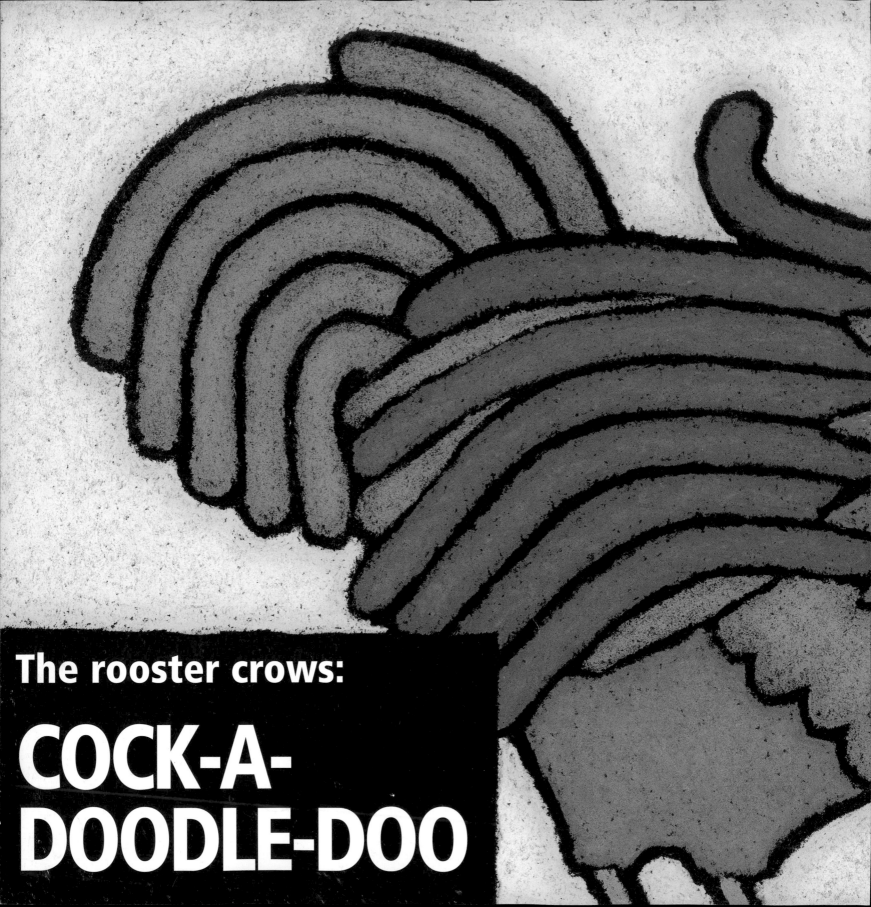

The rooster crows:

COCK-A-DOODLE-DOO

French **COCORICO**

Swedish **KUCKELIKU**

Icelandic **GAGG-A-LA-GÚ**

In Romany I say:

KIKIRIKI

In Russian I say:

КУД-КУД

The hen clucks:

CLUCK

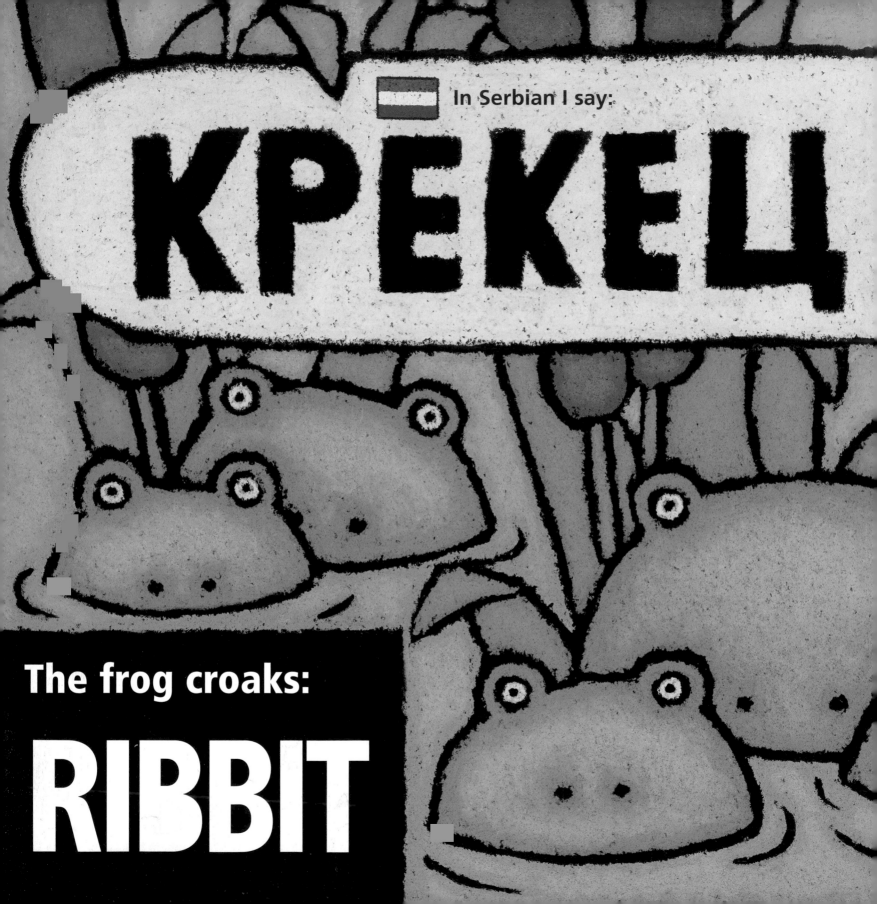

The elephant toots:
TOOT

In Swahili I say:
TOOTS

First published in Ljubljana, Slovakia, by Mladinska knjiga Založba
under the title *Animals' International Dictionary*.
Published in the United States, Great Britain and Canada in 2006
by North-South Books, an imprint of NordSüd Verlag AG, Gossau Zürich, Switzerland.

Distributed in the United States by North-South Books Inc., New York.
Library of Congress Cataloging-in-Publication Data is available.
A CIP catalogue record for this book is available from The British Library.

ISBN-13: 978-0-7358-2058-6
ISBN-10: 0-7358-2058-9

1 3 5 7 9 10 8 6 4 2
Printed in Belgium

Cat	Dog	Bird
MEOW	WOOF WOOF	CHIRP CHIRP
MIAW	WWFF WWFF	TSIRP TSIRP
MEEGAW MEEGAW	WUF WUF	TSEEP TSEEP
ΝΙΑΟΥ ΝΙΑΟΥ (NIAOU NIAOU)	ΓΑΒ ΓΑΒ (GAW GAW)	ΤΣΙΟΥ ΤΣΙΟΥ (TSIOU TSIOU)
MIAO	BAU BAU	CIP CIP
MIAU MIAU	WAU WAU	TSKIF TSKIF
MIAOU	OUAH OUAH	CUI CUI
MIAU	GUAU GUAU	PIO PIO
MEW MEW	BUB BUB	PIU PIU
MIAU	ARU ARU	FIU FIU
MIAU	HAM HAM	CIRIP CIRIP
MYOU MYOU	VOFF VOFF	BEE BEE
MYAU MYAU	VOFF VOFF	KVIRREVITT
MIAEU MIAEU	VOEU VOEU	PIP PIP
MYAU MYAU	VOFF VOFF	KVITTER KVITTER
MIAUW MIAUW	WAF WAF	TYILP TYILP
MIAHU MIAHU	WOOF WOOF	TYEEP TYEEP
MIOW MIOW	VOW VOW	TSKIRP TSKIRP
ŅAU ŅAU (NAU NAU)	FAU FAU	PĪ PĪ (PEE PEE)
MIAU MIAU	CHAU CHAU	ĆWIR ĆWIR (CHWIR CHWIR)
MŇAU (MNYEOO MNYEOO)	HAF HAF	TRILILI TRILILI
MEYAF	HOV HOV	ČIV ČIV (CHIV CHIV)
MEYOO	AW AW	ČIV ČIV (CHIV CHIV)
МЈАУ (MYAU)	АВ АВ (AW AW)	ЋИЈУ ЋИЈУ (TSKIYU TSKIYU)
МЯУ МЯУ (MIOW MIOW)	БАУ БАУ (BOW BOW)	ЧИК ЧИРИК (TSKIK TSKIK)
МЯУ (MAOO MAOO)	ГАВ ГАВ (GAV GAV)	ЧИК ЧИРИК (TSKIK TSKIK)
МЯУ (MAOO MAOO)	ГАВ ГАВ (GAV GAV)	ЦВІРК ЦВІРК (TSVIRK TSVIRK)
МЯВ МЯВ (MYAV MYAV)	КУФ КАФ (CUF-CAF)	ЦИЙ ЦИЙ (TSIY TSIY)
MYOW MYOW	AUH AUH	SIRTS SIRTS
MIOW	HOW HOW	TSIRP TSIRP
MIOW MIOW	FOW FOW	CSIRIP CSIRIP
MIYAF	HOF HOF	ČIV ČIV (EF EF)
מיאו (MIAOU)	הב-הב (HAF HAF)	ציף ציף (TSIF TSIF)
مواء (MUVAA)	نباح (NUBAAH)	زقزقة (SAKSAKA)
ميو (MIOW)	هاپ هاپ (HAP HAP)	جیک جیک (DSCHIK DSCHIK)
म्याउ म्याउ (MIAU MIAU)	कुकुर भुक्छ (VUK VUK)	ची ची (TSCHI TSCHI)
喵 (MIAO)	呒 呒 (OW OW)	唧 唧 (DTSHE DTSHE)
ニャーオ (NYAHO)	わんわん (WANG WANG)	チュンチュン (TSCHUNG TSCHUNG)
เหมียว เหมียว (MEOW MEOW)	โฮ่ง โฮ่ง (HONG HONG)	จิ๊บ จิ๊บ (TSCHIP TSCHIP)
NGEAU	KOONG KOONG	CICIP
NYAUUU NYAOUUU	WOOK WOOK	CHIRP CHIRP

COOK-A-DOODLE-DOO	CLUCK CLUCK	REBBIT REBBIT
CWC-A-DWDL-DW	CLWC CLWC	RIBIT RIBIT
A-KAHIK-AAIRIGEE-AAIRIGEE	POC POC	RIBID RIBID
KIKIPIKOY KIKIPIKOY	KOKOKO KOKOKO	ΚΟΥΑΞ ΚΟΥΑΞ (KUAKH KUAKH)
CHICCHIRICHI	COCCODE	GRA GRA
CHICHERICHI	GOH GOH GOH GOH	QUAC QUAC
COCORICO	COT-COT-CODAK	COA COA
KIKIRIKI	COC-CO-CO-COC	CRUA CRUA
KIKKIRIKI	CAWC CAWC	RAWC RAWC
CAW-CAW-CAW RAW-CAW	CAW CAW	REBIT REBIT
CUCURIGU	COTCODAC COTCODAC	OAC OAC
GAGG-A-LA-GOO	GAGG GAGG GAGG	KVAKK KVAKK
KYKKELIKY	KLUKK KLUKK	KVEKK KVEKK
KYKLIKY	BOK BOK	KVEK KVEK
KUCKELIKU	KLUCK KLUCK	KVACK KVACK
CKUCKELECKU	TOCK TOCK	KVAAK KVAAK
KOKKEDOODDELDOO	KLOOK KLOOK	KVUK KVUK
KIKERIKI KIKERIKI	TACK TAAAK TAAAK	QUAK QUAK
KI KE RI GŪ (KI KE RI GOO)	KU-KU-DĒ (KU KU DE)	KVĀ KVĀ (KFAH KFAH)
KOOKOORYKOO	KO KO	REHOO-REH ALBOH KOOMKA KOOM KOOM
KYKYRYKÝ (KIKIRIKI)	KOKODAHK	KVAK KVAK
KIKIRIKI	KOKODAK	REGA REGA KVAK
KUKURIKU	KOKOKO	KRE KRE
КУКУРИК (KUKURIKU)	КО КО ДА (KO-KO-DA)	КРЕКЕЦ КРЕКЕЦ (KREKEZ KREKEZ)
КУКУРИГУУ (KUKURIGUU)	КО КО КО (KO-KO-KO)	КВАК КВАК (KVAK KVAK)
КУ КА РЕ КУ (KOO-KA-RE-KOO)	КУД КУДА (KOOD-KOODA)	КВА КВА (KVA KVA)
КУ КА РЕ КУ (KOO-KA-RE-KOO)	КУД КУДА (KOOD-KOODA)	КВА-КВА (KVA KVA)
КУКОРЕ (KUKORE)	КЯР КЯР (KYAR KYAR)	ВАТОР ВАТОР (VATOR VATOR)
KI-KE-RIKII	KA-KA-KAA	KROOKS KROOKS
KUKKO KIEKUU	KOT KOT	KUR KUR
KUKURIKOW	KOT-KOT-KOTKODAHCS	BREKEKE
KEKEREKE	KOKODAK	REHGA KFAK
קוקוריקו (KUUKUUREKUU)	קוד קודה (KOD KODA)	קווא קווא (KVA KVA)
صياح (SIYAAH)	قاقت (KAKAT)	نقيق (NAKEEK)
قوقولی قوقو (GHOO-GHOOYE-GHOO-GHOO)	قد قد قدا (GHOD-GHOD-GHODA)	قورررر قوررر (GHOOR GHOOR)
कुखुरीकाह (KUKHURIKA)	काऽ काऽ (KHA KHA)	टररर टररर (TRRR TRRR)
喔 喔 (VU VU)	咯 咯 (GE GE)	呱 呱 (GOOA GOOA)
コッケコッコー (KOKKE-KOKKOH)	コッコ (KOKKO)	ケロッケロッ (KEROKKEROK)
ไก่ขัน (EK-E-EK-EK)	กุ๊ก กุ๊ก (KUK KUK)	อ๊บ อ๊บ (OB OB)
KOKOK	KETOOK-KETAK	KOOAK
KOKOLIKOOO	CLAK CLAK CLAK	CROAAAAAKK